ON THE PLUS SIDE

P.A. KURCH

An imprint of Enslow Publishing

WEST **44** BOOKS™

Please visit our website, www.west44books.com.
For a free color catalog of all our high-quality books,
call toll free 1-800-542-2595 or fax 1-877-542-2596.

Cataloging-in-Publication Data

Names: Kurch, P.A.
Title: On the plus side / P.A. Kurch.
Description: New York : West 44, 2020.
Identifiers: ISBN 9781538385173 (pbk.) | ISBN 9781538385180
  (library bound) | ISBN 9781538385197 (ebook)
Subjects: LCSH: Teenage pregnancy--Juvenile fiction. | Pregnant
  teenagers--Juvenile fiction. | Life change events--Juvenile fiction.
Classification: LCC PZ7.1.K873 Wa 2020 | DDC [F]--dc23

First Edition

Published in 2020 by
Enslow Publishing LLC
101 West 23rd Street, Suite #240
New York, NY 10011

Copyright © 2020 Enslow Publishing LLC

Editor: Caitie McAneney
Designer: Seth Hughes

Photo Credits: Cover (pregnancy test) Africa Studio/
Shutterstock.com; cover (calendar) mizar_21984/Shutterstock.com.

Printed in the United States of America

CPSIA compliance information: Batch #CW20W44: For further information contact
Enslow Publishing LLC, New York, New York at 1-800-542-2595.

For Yazenid

CHAPTER **ONE**

There I was.

Bryan Parker. The smart kid. The quiet kid. The polite kid. The kid who was always asked to help out. Even though I was only seventeen years old, people always said I was going places.

I never got into trouble. I kept to myself. Getting into trouble would've killed me. It would've killed my teachers, too. And my parents! If I ever got in big trouble with them, well...

My parents raised me to be responsible. They taught me to admit my mistakes and fix them. I always did that, without fail. My mother was tough on me. She grew up in Korea with a big family. She wanted me to go to college, something that she never got to do. And my dad! He had been to several colleges. Right now, he was even teaching at one.

As a kid, I knew I wanted to be smart. Just like him. So I stuck to school and excelled at everything I did. By seventeen, I applied to college. I was going to make video games someday. I was sure of it, and I was counting down the months until graduation and *life starting*.

But then I'd remember my boring, quiet life in the suburbs. I loved the idea of living in a big city. It was always busy and loud. I could never be bored there.

I was an only child and for good reason. My mom had nine brothers and sisters. My dad had four. They loved the idea of a simpler life. They also loved having their attention all on me—their one child.

My dad's parents were very tough on him growing up. He wasn't allowed to make mistakes. He couldn't get into trouble. So when I was born, he knew that he wanted different for me, and he would tell me this all the time. "Don't ever be afraid to come to me," he'd say. "No matter how much trouble you find yourself in, Bryan."

I know I did well. I stayed out of trouble. I kept a small circle of friends. I made my parents happy.

Sometimes, my mom would get in a mood where she'd yell at me. Maybe my essay for school wasn't quite finished. She was very serious about school. I'd sit there and listen to her lecture me, and then my dad, minutes later, would come to my door. "Don't worry about it," he'd say.

He knew it was okay to take breaks sometimes. He'd invite me into the living room to play video games for a while. My mom would sigh, telling him it was waste of time. My dad would then very gently remind her, "He's only a kid once, Jin."

The argument would end there. "Well. Maybe just for today," she'd say. She knew I needed a break from schoolwork and a quiet life. And that's how it went, for years.

✚

Alyssa Holbrook and Evan O'Reilly were my two best friends. Alyssa and I started dating when we were juniors. I had known her since kindergarten. She loved everything about law and politics. She wanted nothing more than to become a lawyer. I swear, with her brains and attitude, she could be president.

And Evan! He was a year behind us. He was the most lovable geek I ever knew. Comic books were his *life*.

Sometimes all three of us would play video games together. Those nights weren't complete without lots of junk food. My mom would tell us how she hated junk food. Still, though, she'd buy it for us. She knew we were safer inside. Away from all of the trouble happening *outside*.

And we kept out of trouble. For the most part. I never said we were perfect.

I was a senior now. October had just started. Evan was finding his way through his junior year.

And Alyssa? Alyssa had recently moved a whole town over with her moms and little sister, Laura. She was now in an all-girls school, and she absolutely hated it. The only thing she *did* like was being on Student Council. She put all of her political knowledge to the test. Still, though, she missed being in school with us. We didn't see each other as much, either. Her mom had also recently divorced her dad and remarried. Alyssa hadn't been taking things well.

On top of that, she'd just had a family wedding in Virginia. She had been gone for two weeks and was missing us even more. All of us had school in the morning, too. Her moms, though, started driving back a little too late. We texted back and forth, but that night, she sounded annoyed. She was quieter than usual, too. I didn't think much of it. Not at the time, at least.

Evan and I were in my room as we played games. Time passed slowly. We waited to hear from Alyssa. Just something to know that she got home safely.

The conversations that Evan and I had were usually stupid. That night, though, was different.

Our talk was more serious. The questions were largely for me—my plans for work and school and Alyssa. Graduation was eight months away. And poor Evan! He still had another year. He didn't hide his jealousy well. Or at all.

"Don't you get it!?" Evan yelled. "You're getting out soon!"

I shook my head. "It's not like we're in a prison!" I replied.

Evan disagreed. "School *seems* like a prison," he mumbled.

We talked about other seniors in my class. Some just didn't care anymore. Not me, though. I kept busy. There was no room for mistakes. I just *had* to get into college so I could get out of here. I secretly worried about Evan. He had two older brothers who were super tough on him. Me and Alyssa were his only friends. Without us, he'd be lost. High school wouldn't be the same for him next year.

Flashes of color lit up my room. Suddenly, we stopped talking, as we focused on our game. Finally, Evan spoke.

"So what happens? After college?" he asked. His eyes were locked on my TV. My eyes didn't move, either.

"California. Maybe Toronto," I answered. "That's where the best games are made." I thought about my dream life for a moment. I lost my focus on the game. I stopped playing. I let Evan win.

He glanced at me, half happy, half annoyed, and he set his controller down.

"I don't know what I'm doing yet," Evan said, almost sadly.

"You've still got time," I replied. "You have a whole 'nother year!"

Evan threw up his hands. "Easy for you to say!" he shot back. "You've had your life planned out since, like, fourth grade."

"First grade, actually," I joked. "And I get your point."

My phone buzzed. Alyssa's name appeared on the screen. Evan knew it was her.

"And you two," he said. "You've liked *her* since the fourth grade."

I laughed. "Wrong again, Evan. Kindergarten, at least."

Evan picked up his controller. He handed me mine. I told him to wait a second.

CHAPTER **TWO**

Alyssa

i am soooo happy to be coming home

i miss u guys

we miss you too

when will you be home?

hopefully sometime this year

just passed through new york

so a couple more hours

how was Virginia?

boring, actually

everyone in this car is driving me crazy

and i think i rly messed things up

i want to see u

after school tomorrow

how so

did you get into a fight with your mom again?

and sure

is everything ok

?

I love you.

love you too

That's where the conversation ended. Maybe she fell asleep? I texted her one last thing. Maybe she would see it.

be safe.

Her words, though. They burned in the back of my mind. "Messed things up." I kept going over it. Evan could tell that I wasn't focused. At *all*.

"Dude, why aren't you playing?" he asked. He sounded annoyed. His eyes stayed glued to the screen. Evan continued pressing buttons. He swore and then he sighed. "What did Alyssa want?"

I shrugged my shoulders. "She's on her way home," I replied. "But the trip. I don't think it went well."

"Is it her moms again?"

"I don't know. Maybe," I replied. Evan paused the game.

Now, Evan *never* pauses his games. The house could be on fire and I swear he'd still play. He looked at me, with this serious look on his face. "What did she say?" he asked.

I showed him my phone. He read the texts silently to himself. He shook his head and grabbed his controller. Evan un-paused the game. "Bryan, it's probably just her moms again," he told me. "Plus, Alyssa misses her dad. This is all sorta new to her."

Evan seemed so sure. I still had a weird feeling. Evan handed me my controller. "Now, please," he went on. "We have a boss to beat. I can't do it alone."

I played for only about a minute. And then, out of nowhere, I asked him, "Why would Alyssa want to see *me* about *her* moms?"

Evan continued playing. He barely moved. Did he hear me?

"Evan," I said. He was ignoring me. I knew him

too well. I called his name again. Then I took *my* controller and paused the game.

Evan dropped his controller onto the floor. He swore again, and he looked down, putting his face into his hands. "She said she messed up. And what? She needs to see you? After school?" he asked.

"Well, no," I corrected him. "She wants to see me. *Wants.* She didn't say *needs.*"

He glared at me. I knew that he knew about Alyssa and me. And what happened right before she moved away.

"That party we had right before school started," he continued. "You two disappeared for an hour. Nobody knows where you two went."

I wondered for a moment. Should I play stupid? Nothing got by him, though. Alyssa and I did disappear for a while at the party. Evan didn't mention it at the time, so why bring it up now? Did he know what happened? I decided to play it off as nothing. "*Half* hour," I shot back. "And I told you. It was just for a walk."

Evan thought about it, but I don't think my plan worked. He shook his head. "Look," he said, as he started his game again. "You'll see what happens after school tomorrow. It's probably nothing."

He was probably right. Plus, it was late. We were both tired. We didn't talk much after that. Eventually I fell asleep. I think Evan played games through the night.

+

Staying up late to play video games was not the brightest idea. Mondays are tough enough as it is. Evan and I pretty much crawled through the school day.

We never beat that boss, either! Evan ended up crashing on my couch. I hadn't slept long. I mostly sat wide awake in my bed. Alyssa's text kept bothering me all night. Sometimes, throughout the day, I'd be happy about being in class. It kept my mind off of things. And then, I'd suddenly remember Alyssa's text, and things felt worse all over again.

After school, I walked alone to the bookstore, where Alyssa asked me to meet her. That was one of our favorite spots to hang out. Me, her, and Evan usually spent hours there after school.

Alyssa's favorite books were about human rights. She would read books about women's rights and famous activists. And Evan loved the comic book section. He would explain things to me that I just never understood. I myself loved gaming magazines. I knew one day I wanted to be in one.

Today, though, there'd be none of that. I think Alyssa just wanted to talk. Evan asked if I wanted him to tag along. "Not today, buddy," I told him.

He told me he understood.

It was a much colder October day than usual. My walk was quiet. All I had were my thoughts. Lots of thoughts. That's all I remember now. That, and Halloween decorations that lined every front yard.

Eventually I turned the corner where the bookstore was. I saw Alyssa standing outside, holding her coat close to her. She didn't see me. She was looking down at her phone. I called her name. She looked up and smiled, but only briefly. She looked a little worried. I couldn't even get out a full "hello." She gently grabbed my arm and marched me right into the bookstore.

The owner, Mr. Jennings, said "hi" to us. "And Bryan," he said, "tell Evan! A whole bunch of new comic books just came in!" I promised I'd tell him. "You're good kids," Mr. Jennings said. Alyssa was in a hurry. She tried pulling me away without seeming rude.

She and I walked between the shelves of books. "So how was vacation?" I asked. A new magazine caught my eye. I stopped myself.

"Fine. Wonderful, even," she replied. Her answer was short, almost sharp.

"And how was school?"

"I didn't go today. We didn't get home until two in the morning."

Alyssa eventually stopped answering my

questions. Her lips were sealed. I started to worry. Did what we *did* together ruin everything? The move wouldn't have helped, either. We barely saw each other since then.

Finally I asked her, somewhat annoyed: "Is everything... okay?"

It dawned on me that she'd stopped walking. I looked up, realizing where she'd led me. We were standing in the parenting section. Colorful books towered over us. *The Big Baby Name Book!* That one stood out to me for some reason.

I looked at the title. I looked at Alyssa. She looked at the same book. Our eyes locked. And then, out of nowhere, she fell into my arms, crying.

"Woah, take it easy," I said. Bad idea. She began crying even harder. I stood there, awkwardly, as she sobbed. Another couple walked into the same section and they stopped right in their tracks. They looked at me, eyeing me up like I hurt her or something.

"It's just allergies," I told them. They shook their heads at me and turned right around. I felt eyes on us, from around every bookshelf corner. I could've died right there! Right next to the *Just For Dad* magazines. I asked Alyssa to look up at me.

"Can we maybe do this somewhere else?" I asked. She nodded, wiping away her tears.

CHAPTER **THREE**

I offered to drive Alyssa's car to her new house. She was too upset to drive—by what, I still wasn't sure. When we got there, Alyssa quietly opened the door. Their new house was beautiful. I had no time to admire it, though. Alyssa took me by the arm again and headed for the stairs. Her mom called her name. Alyssa cringed. Slowly we walked back downstairs. I looked around more this time. There were boxes everywhere. They were still unpacking.

"Hi, Bryan," her mom said to me with a smile. "Dinner's almost ready, Alyssa," she continued. "You're welcome to join us, Bryan."

Alyssa squeezed my arm. I knew what that meant. Keep my mouth *shut*. "No, Mom," Alyssa replied. "He just stopped by. To get his... books! Books that I forgot to give back to him. Before we moved."

My heart was racing. I could feel how nervous

Alyssa was. Her mom looked at us like something was off. I prayed that she didn't ask for the titles of these imaginary books. She finally smiled. "Okay. No problem," she said. "Dinner's in half an hour!"

Alyssa glared at me. "Too close," she whispered. We raced up the stairs again and right into her room. She told me to sit down at her desk. Alyssa closed the door, leaving it open just a bit. She then walked to her dresser and opened the bottom drawer. Clothes fell to the floor. Alyssa tossed them aside.

Then, something landed by my feet. *Two* somethings. Two long pieces of white plastic.

I knew exactly what they were. My jaw dropped.

Alyssa crossed her arms. Her face grew red and her lip shook in a way I had rarely seen in all of our years as friends. She choked back a sob. I knew she didn't want anyone to hear. Alyssa started to walk back and forth, talking to herself. "My moms are going to kill me," she said. To be fair, Alyssa always said that, no matter what she did. But this time? They might *actually* kill her. I picked up the pregnancy tests. I rubbed my eyes.

Both of them read "Pregnant." And right there, next to that word: a big, blue plus sign. Maybe I was seeing things. I looked at one more closely. Maybe it wasn't a plus sign? The room was dark and dusty from all of the unpacking. Only evening light shone through the curtains. I tried to focus my eyes. No, it was definitely a plus sign. I dropped the first one on the desk. I checked the second one.

I couldn't breathe for a minute. My whole future, my dreams of school and video games and life in a big city, crumbled away in my mind. In that instant, everything changed. Alyssa approached her desk. She snatched the pregnancy test out of my hand.

She stared at it for what felt like hours. She wiped tears from her eyes.

"What did we do?" Alyssa asked, almost in a whisper. "What *do* we do?" she continued. I could hear her anger and disbelief and shame. All of that in *herself*. I myself was running through emotions—hundreds of them.

I stammered. Hesitated. And then: "We've gotta tell someone." I didn't believe what I just said. Not at first. I looked at Alyssa. "Right?" I asked. My parents would definitely kill me, too. This was too much trouble for being my first *trouble*.

Alyssa picked up the pregnancy tests. She tossed them back into the bottom drawer. Clothes were carelessly piled back on top of them. "No.

We don't tell anyone. *Can't* tell anyone."

"What else are we going to do?" I asked desperately through clenched teeth. This was stupid, thinking we could hide it! I realized I was angry with Alyssa, for the first time in twelve years. We couldn't just *hide* it.

My heart was racing. A child was not part of our plans. I hated myself for thinking that. Years of dreams gone, because of a few minutes of bad judgment. But I knew we had no money and no other plan. I thought of the best answer. "There's always adoption," I told her.

Alyssa looked at me. "Oh cut it out, Bryan," she replied in disgust. She turned away. It all hit her again. "How could we be so stupid? What were we thinking!?" she cried. "I can't have this baby. *Won't* have this baby. And *we* can't have this baby. We want college. Good-paying jobs. We want a *life*! This wasn't supposed to be a part of that! We need to take care of this, like, yesterday."

I stood up from the desk. I put my head in my hands. I knew what she was getting at—getting rid of the baby altogether. And even though I didn't want it, I didn't know that I wanted *that*. "Let's not decide on anything now. Please?" I begged her. She didn't answer me. I begged her again. She nodded, but I knew she didn't mean it.

"I'll drive you home," she told me. I went in for a kiss, but she turned away.

Alyssa grabbed two books from her nightstand. I looked at the covers. They weren't my books. "Just in case my parents see us," she said.

CHAPTER **FOUR**

My dad called me downstairs. He had called for me about four times. I just laid in my bed in the darkness. My face was buried in my pillow. Should I scream? Cry? Nothing came out. I just felt guilty. Terrified. My stomach was in knots. How could I break it to them? What was Alyssa going to do? There was a knock on my door.

"Bryan, man," my dad said. He cracked the door open. "Dinner's been ready."

Blinding light from the hallway filled my room. I squinted my eyes.

"You feeling okay?" he asked as he approached me. He put his hand on my forehead. "You're kind of warm."

I didn't answer him. "Get some rest," he said. He closed my door as he walked out. "I'll check on you soon."

I really did feel sick. I didn't sleep. There was no way I could. And Alyssa! I knew I couldn't change her mind. After all, *she's* the one who had to carry it. It? The baby. *She* was the one who had to give birth. Any decision I made would be nothing. It would just be an opinion. Still, I felt like I was being choked by responsibility for the situation.

Evan texted me twenty times. I never responded. Eventually he stopped. An eternity passed. Sunlight eventually filled my room. I got up for school that morning. I wore the same shirt from yesterday.

This continued all week. I didn't eat anything. I didn't talk to anybody. I thought about calling Alyssa. I considered talking to my guidance counselor, Julie (yeah, we were on a first-name basis). Or my dad, at least. Even Evan. I fought with it for days. I almost pressed the call button. Almost knocked on that door. Almost talked to my dad in his office.

Suddenly, it was Friday.

I sat on the bleachers in gym that day. I forgot my gym clothes for the first time in my life. My gym teacher, though, was very understanding. He told me not to worry. And then Evan—freaking Evan! He, too, "forgot" his clothes. Guess who joined me on the bleachers?

He sat on the bench right behind me. We watched as the class played dodgeball. He didn't talk to me for a while. Eventually I felt him lean in. "Why have you been ignoring me? And my texts?" he asked. His eyes were still on everyone else. I didn't answer. "What did Alyssa say?"

I didn't want to think about it. My silence must have been enough.

He sighed. "What did they always teach us, Bryan? In health class?"

I felt my body freeze up. Health class? Did he know? Suddenly, I wanted to punch him. *Too many witnesses, though*, I thought.

Evan patted my shoulder. "They taught us everyone needs a support system. So I'm here if you need me," he said. I felt my shoulders relax. "I hope you know that."

The bell rang and we both jumped to our feet. I tried so hard to lose him in the hallway rush. Suddenly, Principal Stevenson appeared, towering over everyone. He was stepping out of his office. "Bryan Parker!" he shouted.

My dad was standing right behind him.

CHAPTER **FIVE**

My dad's face was red. He told Principal Stevenson I was leaving early. I followed my dad to the car. My heart was pounding. I opened the door and got inside. My dad went to start the car, but he just held his keys in the ignition. He stared out ahead. My throat was too tight to swallow.

"Alyssa's parents called me early this morning," he finally began. "Her sister found something of hers, and Alyssa didn't deny it."

After a week of bottling it up, I fell apart. Right there in my dad's car *in the school parking lot.* "Does Mom know?" I asked, fearing the answer.

My dad nodded. "She's with Alyssa's parents right now. Mom's taking it kind of hard." He let out the biggest sigh. "What did I always tell you, Bryan?" he asked. For a split second, he sounded angry. That hurt the most.

"I know, Dad, I know," I cried.

"I'm not mad," he told me. "I'm just upset that

you didn't come to me."

I felt like the biggest failure as a son. As maybe even a soon-to-be father. "I wanted to tell you," I admitted. "But that's a lot! For anyone!" I must have sounded like a mess, my voice cracking. My dad told me to stop and calm down.

My dad's face turned grim. "Alyssa doesn't want to," he said. "Have the baby, I mean." He sounded worried. "They're all having a very serious talk right now. You need to be there."

My heart ached. My dad looked at me. He looked like *he* was about to cry.

"You both have your futures planned," he said. "I mean, you making video games and Alyssa going to law school. You've both worked toward that for years!" he continued. "But you're both still young. And now you both have to grow up quickly."

I kept wiping my tears away.

"It's not the end of the world," he said. "Mistakes happen. Mistakes are fixable. And we're all here to support you guys. You two owe that child *something*," he finished. I didn't know what to do with what he said. On one hand, the baby was a mistake. On the other hand, we owed it something?

"Yeah, Dad," I replied.

He started the car. I pressed my forehead

against the window. *What did I get everyone into?* I thought. I kept my eyes on the passing houses, cars, and trees. I couldn't stand looking at my dad.

Deep down, I knew he was heartbroken.

I was, too.

CHAPTER **SIX**

My heart pounded as we walked up Alyssa's driveway. I knocked on the door and Alyssa answered, her eyes red from crying. As soon as I walked in, she gave me the biggest hug. I looked at her moms. I was surprised they could even look at me.

And then I saw my mom. I almost expected her to yell at me in front of everyone.

It wouldn't have been the first time. But she just stood up and held out her arms. She hugged me quickly and then took a step back. She looked at me, sadly, and then she just sort of smiled, like everything might be all right. I swear, I never loved that woman more.

I sat down next to Alyssa. I held her hand the entire time. We both started by taking responsibility for everything. Alyssa then told me how they'd been talking all morning. "I think we should do this, Bryan," she told me.

"Do...?" I asked stupidly.

"Have the baby."

It took me a second, but I knew it was what I wanted, too. I held her hand even tighter.

And then our parents had questions. Tons of them. Tough ones.

"When did this happen?" her parents wanted to know.

"Why didn't you tell us right away?" my mom asked.

"What were you thinking?" my dad asked. And then, the biggest question: "And how are you two going to make this right?"

It was the toughest half hour of *my life*. Once that was over, the real conversations began. Things got easier after that.

"Stay in school!" my parents begged us. Our moms told Alyssa what to expect in the coming months. Oh, and details about labor and giving birth. My dad turned pale. I'm pretty sure that I did, too. Alyssa nudged me.

Alyssa sometimes started to get upset. I tried to calm her down. We talked about everything we needed to do. "What about money? For clothes, toys, diapers, food, and a crib?" her mom asked. Alyssa's stepmom got angry with herself. "I just got rid of Laura's old crib, too!"

My dad hadn't been saying much. He sat in

a chair across from us in deep thought. I knew what he was doing. He was adding up all of the prices in his head. Judging by the look on his face, it wasn't good. He noticed me watching. My dad winked at me as if to say, *We're going to be okay.*

I knew I had to start working immediately. "The bookstore!" Alyssa said. "You spend enough time there." I agreed—surely I could take some hours after school. It would be *some* money, at least. Alyssa promised to take up more hours at the store at the mall she hated. "Until I can't anymore," she said.

Our focus turned to school. Alyssa seemed tense as we figured out the timeline. The baby would be here just in time for graduation. I know she wanted to walk across the stage, but she would be *very* pregnant by then. "Everyone's going to judge me!" she cried.

Her moms told her not to worry about it. Alyssa turned to me. "And you! You'll have it so easy!" she said. "No one in your school will ever know. My belly will be as big as a watermelon by then!" She put her left hand on my stomach. She stared at it and then pulled it away.

And then she began *sobbing.* I couldn't calm her down from this one.

Her parents rushed to the couch we were sitting on. I stood up and moved out of their way.

My guilt hit the roof. I must have looked so weird standing there. I felt useless.

Alyssa's little sister Laura appeared at the bottom of the stairs. All that crying had woken her up from her nap. She had a baby doll in one hand as she rubbed her eyes with the other. Laura then did what she did best. She *herself* started crying. Her two moms jumped up and ran to her. Laura made the biggest scene she could. I thought I saw Laura flash a smile at her sister.

"I swear, people!" Alyssa screamed. My mom jumped. "I better not have a girl! This world doesn't need another *Laura*!"

CHAPTER **SEVEN**

Turns out, I didn't even have to tell Evan about the pregnancy. It almost bugged me that he figured it out just from how Alyssa and I were acting. One night, a text came from him.

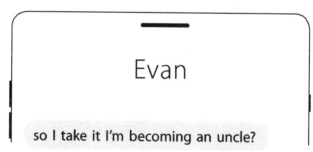

Evan

so I take it I'm becoming an uncle?

That meant the world to me. I needed him around. I called him and told him about *everything*. And then I told him how much I needed a job. "I need one, too!" he said. "I'll get one with you!" It was decided. We'd go there right after school tomorrow.

Mr. Jennings greeted us at the door. I asked him about working part-time and weekends. He hired me on the spot. No questions asked! "You've been coming here for years," he said to me. "I've always said you were a good kid, Bryan."

I didn't feel like a good kid. I had a child on the way. I wasn't about to tell Mr. Jennings that, though. What would he think? The idea of working, though, made me feel better. Like I had some control in this new situation. Mr. Jennings even offered a job to Evan. "I'll let you work in the comic book section!" he told him with a laugh.

Evan didn't miss a beat. He swore in excitement and apologized immediately. "I accept your offer with the greatest honor, sir." Evan said. He gently bowed to Mr. Jennings. I shook my head in embarrassment.

"I'll see you boys tomorrow," Mr. Jennings said. "Welcome aboard."

We started the next day as promised. I enjoyed the evening walks to the bookstore. It allowed me to think and clear my mind. That is, when Evan wasn't talking. He was over the moon about this new "dream job" of his. "Don't you get it!?" he'd say with a hop in his step. "I'll get to read new comic books before anyone else!"

His energy was contagious. I couldn't help but feel happy for him.

✦

There eventually came a day when I was asked to stock parenting books. Every box I opened was a reminder of my new life. What had I done to myself? And Alyssa? Even though I hated the thought of this whole parenting section, I grabbed a book. It was basically a survival guide for first-time parents.

I flipped through it in the break room. I took notes in my head. I cringed at some of the gory details, like how babies' first poops are like dark green tar. It was truly horrifying stuff. The next day, I chose another book. This time, I picked one about what to expect in the baby's first year. Milestones that they would reach every month. My reading continued for days.

It all seemed like so much. So much could go wrong! Problems getting pregnant. (Well, no problem *there*.) Problems during pregnancy. Problems during birth. Allergies. Choking. Toy defects.

I worried a lot. Sometimes I'd feel downright depressed. All of this new info was swimming around in my head.

During dinner, I'd talk to my parents about the book I read that day. I can still hear my mom's words. "There's no instruction book, sweetheart," she'd say. "You learn as a parent. You grow. You make mistakes. You learn from it."

I had made enough mistakes. Enough was enough! I began taking notes as I read. I filled up an entire notebook. I was going to know everything. I mean, I had seven months to learn, right? I was going to be the best I could be for Alyssa and the baby.

✚

At work, I met lots of interesting people. A lot of soon-to-be parents, too. They'd come into the store all scared and nervous like me. Some were excited. And they were *always* older than me. Most of them were married. Most of them had good jobs and even homes. A few couples already had lots of children. I don't know *why*. I mean, one child seemed scary enough, and mine wasn't even here yet!

These parents were always impressed with me. I knew all of the newest books and newest research. I was a know-it-all. "Oh, you need a book about your growing baby? Here's three." Or, "Need to know the best sleep training skills? Here's a whole row of books!"

Mr. Jennings loved me for it. He would tell me every night, "These people can't say enough about you!" Helping others helped *me*. It helped me to remember everything, stay sharp on my baby knowledge. It helped me feel better about things.

Evan made a splash, too. He got the entire Comic Book Club from school to start visiting. Every Thursday after school, they'd order pizzas and buy tons of comics. Mr. Jennings couldn't be happier. He gave Evan and me a raise.

Every payday, I'd buy a parenting book for Alyssa and me. One day, I bought this book called *The Big Book of a THOUSAND Baby Names*. We hadn't talked about names yet. So we sat on her couch and flipped through the pages. We'd make jokes. Alyssa liked a few of the names. She circled her favorites. Her parents asked us what was so funny. They, too, took turns with it.

I took the book home. I circled my favorites.

Evan stopped by that night. Once he saw the book, he totally lost interest in video games. He didn't play once! He just looked through the book. This stupid book! "This is fun!" he said. "It's kind of like choosing a name for a new dog." I told him there was no comparison. And Evan chose weird names. Like names you'd find in a *comic book*. The only normal name he picked was Peter. I was happy with that until he explained it.

"With your last name," he told me in excitement, "he'll be Peter Parker."

I pretended I didn't get it. "Peter Parker? Spiderman? Seriously, Bryan?" he said angrily. I still acted like I had no idea who that was. Evan's face got red. He left my house early that night.

I came home one night after a long day. My mom wasn't in bed like she usually was. No. She was at the dining room table with her reading glasses on. She was looking at the baby name book! She had colored pens and was using them *all*.

My dad was annoyed. "Aren't you coming to watch TV?" he asked. She told him about the book. I wouldn't see that book again for days. And my parents! They never finished their Netflix show.

A week later, the book reappeared on my desk. It was torn. Stained. The pages were filled with hundreds of different-colored circles. I couldn't read most of the names. Whole columns were crossed off. Arrows and scribbles filled the pages. It was a mess.

I was in shock as I looked at the pages. By some miracle, Alyssa and I circled the same two names. Two names out of a thousand! One for a boy and one for a girl.

If it was a boy, Joseph. And if it was a girl, Sara. We knew we wanted to be surprised.

And so it was decided! Alyssa and I high-fived. And then we kissed. She told me how much she loved me. And all was good in the world for literally thirty seconds. Evan then brought up a good point. "The middle names," he said. He seemed confused. "They need middle names, don't they?" he asked.

I looked at Alyssa. I wanted to scream. I told him to get out.

Never again. "I am never opening that book again!" I yelled.

CHAPTER **EIGHT**

School and work took up more time by November. Alyssa's pregnancy kept going, too. We were saving up every dollar and every cent. Slowly, the money began adding up. We knew that we wanted to be ready.

Alyssa's moms were ready, too! They had a spare room that they were painting for the baby. Her mom hated the color, though. "Do you think we should repaint it?" she asked Alyssa. Alyssa asked for my opinion.

I looked around the room. It was a bright, sunny color. I really liked it. Alyssa's stepmom liked it, too, but Alyssa shot me this look. "We'll be right back," Alyssa said. She and her mom disappeared for a short while. They returned with two new gallons of paint.

I offered to do the painting this time. They were already doing so much for me and Alyssa. I needed backup, though. I called up Evan. "Are you free?" I asked him. "For like, an hour? I have to paint."

"Paint what?" he asked. I heard a game in the background. I could tell what game it was, too, just based on the sounds. It was a new game that both of us were going to play together. I never had the time anymore. I suddenly felt sad. Jealous, even.

"The baby's room. Alyssa and her mom hated the color."

"I thought they picked out the color!" Evan shouted. He then got quiet. Really quiet. Sounds of the game continued. I wished I was there playing.

"The color looked too bright when it dried. I just need an hour! Please," I begged. I promised him Chinese food. That's all it took for him.

"I'm on it," he said.

Evan and I got straight to work. We only stopped to eat our dinner. And then we both got the worst headaches. Alyssa's mom marched upstairs. "That paint! It's so strong!" she said. "I can smell it from the kitchen! Let's open a window in here."

She walked to the window and tried to pull it up. She struggled with it. She looked up and down at it, mumbling to herself. She tried a few more times to open it. And then she looked at me and

Evan. "Alright," she snapped. "Who did this one?"

I walked to the window. Embarrassed. I took a good look. Evan had painted over the window's edges. The window was painted shut.

Forever.

CHAPTER **NINE**

By December, Alyssa and I started making our lists of things we needed to buy. I was ready for it, having read all of those books at work. I knew all of the best toys, car seats, and high chairs, but all of them were out of our price range. We started looking elsewhere. We started crossing things off. Putting things back on shelves. Returning things online. We were always looking for something cheaper.

We literally had no other choice, and it *sucked*.

Our parents told us not to worry too much. They, too, wanted the best for the baby. They began surprising us with things. Like the crib Alyssa fell in love with. Or the Super Mario lamp I wanted for the baby's room. I could never pay them back in full. I always offered something. My dad, especially, never wanted the money. "Save it," he told me. "You'll need it." I didn't know what we would do without them.

There was something Alyssa and I both really loved, though. We needed one, too, but not one this fancy or expensive. It was a high-tech video baby monitor. At Christmas, Evan surprised us with it. "I bought this on one condition," he said. "You have to go outside and test this out with me."

I didn't hesitate. "Of course!" I told him.

Alyssa rolled her eyes. "Just please be careful with it," she said. "And be careful with *yourselves!*"

I asked Alyssa's mom where she kept the batteries. Evan and I bundled up and put batteries in the monitor at the same time. We opened the door. There were two feet of snow on the ground. Evan's eyes grew wide.

We stood on the back porch. We tested it to make sure it worked. Evan looked into the camera and he appeared on my screen. "Okay, it works," I told him hurriedly. The wind blew. It was freezing cold. Evan suddenly bolted with the camera piece in hand.

I stared at the screen. All I saw was Evan's nose, sticking out between his hat and scarf. He breathed heavily. He kept quoting lines from *Star Wars*. I laughed like a mad fool. Evan disappeared into the trees. He crouched down, joking that he was spotted by snow monsters.

And then, out of nowhere, he took off again out of the trees. There was a scream and the picture on my screen began spinning. It went dark. I yelled to Evan. A minute later, he appeared in front of me, covered in snow. He was out of breath, telling me, "I dropped it! I tripped in the snow and lost the camera. I can't find it!"

My heart sank. We searched where he fell. The camera, of course, was white. Snow kept falling, making things worse. "We'll never find it, you idiot!" I yelled. We dug like crazy. It was no use.

Evan got on his hands and knees in the snow to look closer. He cringed. "My ankle!" he screamed. "I think I twisted it when I fell!"

I thought he was kidding. Me, being "Friend of the Year," told him to suck it up. We looked for a few more minutes. Evan was close to tears, so I called off the search. He pulled off his boot. His ankle was swollen. I felt so awful.

I carried him back to my house on my back. He quoted more *Star Wars* as I struggled to carry him. I almost left him out there in the cold.

We didn't say a word about the broken baby monitor to anyone. I pretended that I'd put it in a safe place until the baby was born. Alyssa's stepmom helped Evan wrap his ankle. He was being such a drama queen—we had to call his mom.

Months later, in the spring, Alyssa's neighbor called her parents. He ran over something with his riding lawn mower. Nobody knew what it was.

Pieces of glass. White plastic. Metal. All shredded up and spread over his lawn. He wasn't happy. He didn't like kids, especially us. "Surely it's one of Laura's toys. Or a smart phone!" he yelled. Alyssa went next door to take a look. She knew what it was. She texted me and Evan the same thing:

Alyssa

I KNOW WHAT YOU TWO DID LAST CHRISTMAS

Evan called me in a panic. "I don't have the money to replace it, man!" he said. We agreed to go in half on a new one.

They were sold out.

CHAPTER**TEN**

Alyssa called me one night in anger. "My moms!" she told me. "They signed me up for classes!"

"College classes?" I asked. "That's great!"

"No," she scoffed. "Teen parenting classes! What if I see someone? Someone who knows somebody from school? Everyone's going to find out. That'll be it for me!"

I felt awful. "Would it make you feel better if I went to these classes, too?" I asked.

"Wait, they didn't tell you?" she replied with a bitter laugh. "Your parents signed you up, too!"

I hung up on her and flew down the stairs. My parents were setting up for dinner. "Why didn't you guys tell me?" I yelled.

"We were going to tell you during dessert!" my mom yelled back.

+

Alyssa and I started going to class every Tuesday night. I had to miss work those nights, but it was nice to be with Alyssa. We learned a lot of things. We learned about what to expect at the doctor's office and how to keep the baby healthy. It was nice learning it from a person rather than a book.

I asked a lot of questions. The instructors loved me. I don't think the other teen dads appreciated my know-it-all enthusiasm.

We saw a lot of pictures and videos of childbirth. That was... informative, to say the least. I'd start feeling nervous and get all sweaty. Alyssa would laugh at me.

Infant CPR was my favorite class by far. We learned how to save babies from choking. We practiced with these ugly baby dummies. At the end was what is called a skills test. Alyssa dreaded the day of the skills test. I told her, "We've got this!" But she was unsure. Those baby dummies were pretty scary.

We practiced quite a bit. We took notes. We watched the instructor closely. We were going to get this. It came time for our skills test. The instructor, Miss Cheryl, asked me to demonstrate a skill. "Mr. Parker," she said. "Your baby is choking. How do you get the object out of his mouth?"

I picked up the dummy and held it facedown on my forearm. I gently hit its back to get the object out of its mouth. Alyssa was next. She was asked to give the baby rescue breaths.

I could tell Alyssa was nervous—she was actually shaking. She stepped up to our fake baby. She tilted its neck back, ready to perform CPR. We heard a snap. And the baby's head fell off!

The head rolled off the table. It landed on the floor with a loud "crack." Alyssa's jaw dropped. Miss Cheryl looked down at the head. She shook her own head in disappointment. I panicked. She looked back up at us and smiled. "Oh. Oh," she said. "That baby's done, honey. Move on with your lives, sweethearts."

For a second, I thought Alyssa might cry. And then—she broke. I've never heard Alyssa snort before. She had tears in her eyes from laughing so hard. Everyone looked at us.

The teacher signed our papers. She handed them to us.

Somehow, we both passed.

Evan stopped by Alyssa's house to see us that night. We told him all about our CPR baby losing its head and he laughed just as hard as we did. "So what else have they taught you?" he asked.

"Family stuff. And relationship stuff," Alyssa

answered. Evan shook his head.

"What about the basics?" he shouted.

We both looked at him in confusion.

Evan disappeared for a moment. He came back with one of Laura's baby dolls in his hand. Thankfully, Laura was in bed. She didn't like sharing.

"You, Bryan," he said, almost demandingly. "Change his diaper."

"I know how to change a diaper!" I exclaimed. "Besides, we don't even *have* a diaper."

Evan handed one to me. "Where did you..." I started to ask.

"Clock is ticking, Bryan," Evan told me. He showed me the timer counting down on his phone.

Alyssa laughed as I struggled to put the diaper on the doll. It went on backwards, inside out, sideways. "I thought you knew how to do this!" Evan teased.

I was annoyed. "Okay. Maybe this is the one thing I didn't learn in class. Or read in a book," I replied.

He allowed me to try again. This time, though, the diaper ripped. I grew frustrated. Evan looked at Alyssa. "This is just practice, too!" he said. "Besides, it's a clean diaper. The real thing is worse."

I groaned.

"Suck it up, tiger," he laughed.

"Why?" I yelled. "Why are you doing this?"

"Because of Christmas! My ankle was broken!" he shouted.

"You twisted it!" I shot back.

"It was basically broken!" Evan continued.

Our Friday night diaper practice would go on for weeks. Alyssa's parents warned us, somewhat jokingly: "Don't let Laura find out you're using her doll."

We did pretty well hiding the evidence. Until one morning when we forgot to take the practice diaper off of it. Laura found Baby Bink and knew he had been messed with. We never saw Baby Bink again. Or, we never found all of him, at least. We found one of his arms in Laura's sandbox that summer.

Evan held a memorial for Baby Bink the night he disappeared. We sat on the back porch and even had a moment of silence. "We've done all we can, folks," Evan announced. "I think we should cut our losses. Bryan, your diaper changing skills were truly awful. No wonder why Baby Bink disappeared."

I put my head down in embarrassment.

Alyssa raised her hand. "I'll be right back," she said, as she disappeared into the house.

She brought back this torn and very old-looking stuffed giraffe. "Here, Bryan. Practice with this. He was mine when I was a baby."

"I can't do this," I laughed. "It's a giraffe! Get serious."

They begged me. "Oh, you have to, Bryan! Change the giraffe!"

I grabbed a diaper just to shut them up. And would you believe it? I changed it in one try. I got even faster on the next try. Evan made up a chart with markers and stickers. He started to track my progress. Depending on how fast I was, I earned gold, silver, or bronze stars. A gold star meant a kiss—from Alyssa, of course.

I know Evan lied about my time a lot. I got gold stars, all right.

One time. In four weeks.

CHAPTER ELEVEN

On the coldest day of February, a letter arrived from my dream college. I had been accepted!

I'd dreamed of going to school in a big, beautiful city. I'd dreamed of the friends I would make, the games I would design. It was my dream life.

And then reality hit me.

The excitement wore off fast. The baby would be here in four months. I began arguing with myself and everyone else. Could I make it work, going to school on top of being a dad?

Alyssa and I started having arguments. She, too, was accepted into her dream college, but she decided to put that on hold. She *had* to. Besides, she wouldn't move anyways. Her parents wanted her to stick around. And the money! We had saved everything for the baby. There was barely enough to begin with. There definitely wouldn't be anything left for classes or textbooks.

Our plans had to change. They *were* changing.

And it was the hardest thing to accept.

✛

Alyssa's baby bump got bigger day by day. She tried hiding it at school and at work, but it was getting harder to hide behind loose sweatshirts. "People know," she told me. "They stare at me. They talk about me. My hoodie can only cover so much. It's a losing battle."

I looked at her sadly. "People are cruel," I told her. "They're going to talk no matter what's going on."

School was rough for her, too. She was late a lot because of morning doctor's appointments. She couldn't play sports anymore. Her classmates were connecting the dots. The rumors hit hard and fast.

I watched as Alyssa started to withdraw from life. No more going to the mall with friends. No more family dinners at her favorite restaurant. Besides me, Evan, and her moms, Alyssa suddenly had no one to talk to. She grew sad and eventually, quiet. And she grew angry—at herself, the world, and sometimes, me.

On days like that, I tried to cheer her up. I'd talk to the baby. I'd sing songs (very badly). Most times, she'd laugh. She'd smile. She'd hug me.

She'd kiss me. And then, one day, it all stopped working. My jokes. My stories. My love for her. She just shrugged it all off.

"Leave me alone," she begged. "Just for today."

I didn't listen. I tried again. Another hug. Another joke. Alyssa pushed me away, and she sat down at her desk in silence. I called her name but she didn't look at me. I was confused. Hurt, even. I left her house without saying another word.

✚

A gentle breeze blew in the trees that evening. The neighborhood was eerily quiet. "Just for today" turned into a week and my texts went unanswered.

Evan was suddenly quieter than usual, too. And then, just a few days later, during our break at work, Evan told me the news.

"Remember that girl I told you about? From music class?" he asked me. I nodded my head. "She asked me out. I mean, how could I say no?"

"That's great!" I told him. Deep down, though, I knew that was it. He'd be busier now. No more time for video games or hanging out. By the end of the week, I only saw Evan at work. He promised we'd get together soon. "This weekend," he'd say, "or maybe next weekend. I forgot I made plans already."

He always canceled anyways.

Eventually I stopped asking him to hang out. To be honest, neither of us really had time for fun anymore.

CHAPTER **TWELVE**

Parenting classes ended in March. After that, I didn't see Alyssa that much. Sometimes I'd get invited—by her moms—to come over for dinner, but that was it. I went back to working my regular hours. Evan found a different job by the middle of March.

I had nobody now. I hated it. I hated the situation. I started hating *them.*

I started sitting alone in the cafeteria. It was just easier for me to ignore everyone else. And then one day, from the table of girls behind me:

"Guys, didn't you hear? That Alyssa girl who used to go here? She's all knocked up." There were gasps and laughs.

"So, is that why she moved? Because she was sleeping around?" someone asked.

I sat facing away from them, just listening to it all. I didn't eat. I just stared at my lunch.

"I wonder who the father is!" another girl

chimed in. And that's when they started naming people. Popular kids—the football team, the partiers. Once they got through them, the jokes started. They named the kids with no friends. The weird kids. Or the superintendent's son who was always so full of himself. The table roared.

"What about the smart kids? Like Bryan Parker?"

They screamed in laughter. I felt so small.

"It couldn't be him," one of the girls said. "I don't think he even knows what girls *are*."

I think they knew I was sitting nearby. She said it like it was meant for me to hear.

These talks happened for the next few days. I couldn't even stand up for myself.

✛

Work made me feel better. I still liked helping people. I read every new parenting book that came in. I ended up taking more hours to make a little more money. I came home only to sleep. Then I started to fall behind on essays, homework, and studying. My parents and teachers began to worry.

"This isn't like him at all," I heard my mom say to my dad outside my door one night.

I wanted to give up so badly. On everything and everyone.

✦

March crawled by. I caught myself falling asleep during class and gym. My eyelids felt heavy. *Everything* felt heavy. Teachers started to ask to see me after class. I remember having the talks, but I have no idea what they said. I can still see their mouths moving up and down, but no words ever came out. None that I listened to, at least. I was too tired. I nodded my head. I promised to get it together.

Things got so bad that the school tried getting my parents involved. I'd get a text from my dad saying, "We have to talk." I took my time getting home from work. My dinner was always in the fridge waiting for me. Even at home, I started eating alone. In the morning, I would get up earlier than my parents. I barely saw them now.

It was like everyone was upset with me and I was upset with them. I was the teenage son, the best friend, the boyfriend, and the student who messed up. Badly.

I started missing Evan more than ever. I missed our talks. Those stupid talks! Joking with him over superheroes. Arguing all night during boss battles.

I missed Alyssa, too. Losing her absolutely

crushed me. I would try so hard to push things out of my mind. It never worked. Not for long, at least.

All of the stress we faced. Saving money, working long hours, going to school—it was all too much. Plus, it was our first and only real relationship with another person. How on Earth did we know what we were doing?

We were young. *Too young.* There was no way we could've been prepared for any of this. At least, not all of this at once. My dad was right, though.

We had to grow up. We *were* growing up. Way too fast.

CHAPTER THIRTEEN

A couple of weeks later, I was in homeroom when the P.A. system beeped. "Bryan Parker," a voice said. "To the principal's office, please."

I was half asleep on my desk. Someone giggled and teased, "Oooh! Bryan! Now you did it!" I gathered my books. I nearly tripped right over my desk as I stood up. That got more laughs. I rolled my eyes. *Two more months*, I told myself, *and then I'm out of here.*

I sat quietly outside Principal Stevenson's office door. That man made me wait nearly twenty minutes. The door creaked open and I heard the voice of my guidance counselor, Julie. "I just don't know how else to say it," she said.

Principal Stevenson shook his head. He put his hands on his hips and looked down at me. I felt smaller than ever. Some people have that power—it's not a good power to have, but I tell you, it worked. Suddenly, I sat up straight and fixed my shirt. I didn't even feel tired anymore.

He pointed to his office. I knew what that meant. Embarrassed, I stood up and led the way. Julie was standing by his desk. She looked nervous.

"Take a seat, Mr. Parker," Mr. Stevenson told me. My heart began racing. I didn't say a word. *Couldn't* say a word. Julie sat down in the chair next to mine and opened a folder—*my* folder, I guess. She looked at the papers and tried to find something.

The right words. The right tone. The right way to break it to me.

She coughed and cleared her throat. "Bryan," she told me, "we have a problem."

I looked at her. I looked at Principal Stevenson. They stayed quiet. "What?" I squeaked. My mouth was dry.

Principal Stevenson stood up. "Your grades, Mr. Parker," he said as he walked to the front of his desk. He sat down on the edge and crossed his arms. Principal Stevenson then leaned in. "They're bad," he said. "Very bad."

I gulped. "And your college," he continued. "Seems they changed their mind. About *you*."

My heart sank. My head pounded. I saw Julie out of the corner of my eye, wanting to help me. Hug me, even. How many times had we talked about my college dreams? She didn't dare. Not in front of him. Principal Stevenson pointed at the folder that she held in her lap.

Julie sounded nervous. She paused. Stuttered, even. "Your midterms," she began. "The grades. They were lower than usual, especially for you."

I looked at her. Julie didn't look at me, though. She kept her eyes on the paper.

"All of your classes," Julie continued. "Math. Science. English. All of your grades have dropped."

Principal Stevenson stood back up. He circled around Julie and me like a hawk ready to strike. "This college asked us for your grades after the midterms. They didn't like what they saw."

I stared blankly.

"Do you understand, Mr. Parker? They don't want you anymore," he said.

I tried so hard not to break down. It was like *nobody* wanted me anymore. Not Evan. Not my classmates. Not even Alyssa.

So—I walked out.

Principal Stevenson yelled at me to come back. Julie chased after me. She tapped me on my shoulder. I ignored it. She then grabbed my shoulder and spun me around. I stood with her face-to-face.

"What is *going on*, Bryan?" she asked. "Please, tell me! You are so much better than this." I couldn't even look her in the eyes. I was too embarrassed with myself. "I'm sorry," she said. "I should have met with you. *Alone.* Not with that—"

She caught herself before she said something *bad* about Principal Stevenson. My phone buzzed in my pocket. Julie didn't say a word as I took out my phone. It was a text. From Alyssa.

Alyssa

i'm sorry

for pushing you away

but i need to see u

please

don't be mad at me

i'm scared

and nobody's helping

My stomach dropped. I thought about the baby. Something *had* to be wrong. Julie asked me if everything was okay. I shook my head.

"I'm here if you need to talk," she said. "Now go. You're going to be late for your next class."

I walked away feeling so defeated. I texted Alyssa back quickly.

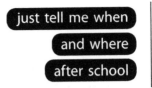

just tell me when

and where

after school

She replied immediately.

i'm not at school

it's a long story

i'll meet you at the coffee shop

next to the bookstore

in an hour

CHAPTER **FOURTEEN**

There were a few hours of school still left. I stood by my locker and stared at my phone. I wondered what to do. I couldn't wait to see Alyssa. *Wouldn't* wait to see Alyssa.

And then something hit me on my back. I knew what it was. It was a ball of paper. Another one hit me. And another. I heard laughing.

I stood there, letting it happen. And then, one of my classmates, a jock named Nate, sneered. "Hey," he told me. "Hey! You! Baby Daddy Bryan!"

How in the world did they find out? In that moment, something inside of me snapped. Everything from the day just came to a boiling point. I turned around. There were three boys standing behind me. I recognized two of the idiots from my homeroom.

I grabbed Nate by the neck of his shirt. "I really wouldn't mess with me right now," I told him through clenched teeth. His friends cheered in glee. Nate begged me to let him go. One of the English teachers, Mr. Swatsworth, saw what was happening. He rushed over to us.

"What is going *on*? Let go of him this instant!" he demanded, so I let go of Nate's shirt. He looked like he was terrified.

I grabbed my backpack from the floor. "Stop right there!" Mr. Swatsworth shouted. I ignored him. I disappeared into the stairwell. I took a deep breath. What just came over me? Who *was* I anymore?

I panicked for a second as I heard someone coming up the stairs. It was Evan! He had his arm around his girlfriend. He didn't even acknowledge me. He just kept walking right past.

Like I was invisible.

That was it. I was *done* for the day. I saw sunlight coming from the bottom of the stairwell. That door! I could do it. I could just walk out. I didn't care about being caught. It's like the father in me came out. I needed to be there—for Alyssa and for our baby.

I looked around before making my move. There was nobody around. I quietly and quickly made my way to the bottom floor. I put my hand on the metal door. It clicked as I pushed it open. *Freedom.* The sun was blinding. I squinted out at the world in front of me. It felt so wrong. It felt so *right*. I walked as fast as I could, far away from that school.

✚

I made it to the coffee shop, my legs burning. I saw Alyssa standing outside. She had this huge gray hoodie on. Nothing could hide her bump at this point, but the sleeves covered her hands. The hood covered her entire face. Any time somebody passed by her, Alyssa looked down. She pulled her hood down even farther, even though it was warm out.

I approached her. We didn't say a word. I looked at her as I held the door open to the coffee shop. Alyssa grabbed me by the fingers. She led me to a corner table, still holding her hood over her face.

I sat down and she followed. She looked around, and then the hood came down. My jaw dropped. Alyssa's left eye was all bruised and purple.

"Who did this to you?" I asked.

"It all started yesterday," she began. "On Student Council."

I reached for her hand. She pulled it away. "Please, Bryan, just let me finish. Everything was going okay. But there's this one girl who *always* opens her mouth. She's been doing nothing but spreading rumors about me." Anger rose up inside of me. "I called her out on it in front of everyone. She was embarrassed. She rolled her eyes and swore at me. But it worked. It shut her up for a while. And then yesterday, in the middle of Student Council, she started with the name-calling. The other girls told her to stop. But things only got worse."

Alyssa's eyes filled with tears. She dried them with her oversized sleeves.

"Did you tell anyone about this?" I asked.

"Of course I did," she replied.

"That's good, right?"

"Well, they kicked her off of Student Council," Alyssa answered. I could tell she was trying to hold back tears. "And then, this morning, she confronted me. She and her stupid friends! They pushed me right up against my locker. They told me to watch my back."

All of this was almost too much to hear.

"There was nobody else around to stop them. So I shoved her back! She fell onto the floor, yelling at me. Her friends helped her up and that's when she hit me. Right in the face."

Alyssa turned, unable to look at me. Her eye looked worse from the side.

"Is this why you're not in school?" I asked.

Alyssa nodded.

"But those girls... they're saying I started it."

"There were others around!" I told her. "How is that right? Who *does* that?"

"It's six against one, Bryan!" she said. "They're making it sound like I made the first move. Principal Stewart says she's looking into it. The security tapes, I mean. But that's not all of it. All of the times I've been late because of doctor appointments, or the times I've missed school because I was sick—they could use that against me."

And then she paused. "They want to suspend me, Bryan. I might miss graduation."

I sat there. Silent. Hurt. I asked her if her parents knew.

"They want to fight it, but they're worried we'll lose. I'm lost, Bryan," Alyssa continued. "I mean, what came over me? Was it just me trying to keep the baby safe? Who *am* I?"

She put her head on the table. She tried so hard not to cry. I reached again for her hand, and this time, she let me hold it.

I confessed to her about my incident in the hallway. How I also got into a scuffle of my own. I told her about my college. And Principal Stevenson being a troll. How Evan ignored me in the hallway. How I just walked away from it all.

And then I had to tell her. How people at *my* school—her old school—knew about the pregnancy.

She broke my heart as she cried. "There's a special hearing with my school board next week," she cried. "I don't know what to do. I want my dad here so badly," she told me. "He's been all over the state with work. Every time I ask to see him he's never around."

I thought about reaching out to him myself.

Alyssa asked me to stay with her, so I did. All afternoon. Eventually, I offered to buy her something to eat. She refused. But me? I ordered myself six chocolate donuts.

I told Alyssa, "Don't judge me! I'm stress eating."

"Welcome to my life," she said, and finally, she smiled.

CHAPTER**FIFTEEN**

A few days later, I decided to skip school. I even called off of work. *Just this once.* My mom didn't even fight me on it. It was my first real day off in months. I crawled into my bed. I swore I would never get out of bed again.

As soon as I got comfortable, my dad called me downstairs. I ignored it, but then my bedroom door flew open. I was shocked by who I saw. It was Evan! With the video game in his hands! The one we were supposed to play together.

"Bryan," he told me. "I have some explaining to do."

I invited him in. Evan started telling me *everything.* He began with his girlfriend. "I told her too many things," he said. "She's a loudmouth! She's been telling everyone about you and Alyssa," Evan said. "It was too late to stop her. I'm sorry. And I know the damage is done, but please! Please forgive me."

I couldn't have cared less at that point. I had missed him too much. "If it makes you feel any better, somebody recorded it—our breakup. It was during music class. It's even online!"

He pulled up the breakup video on his phone. He cringed as we watched. His now ex-girlfriend did not take the breakup too well. It was his first girlfriend, too. That's always the worst.

"And then my mom. My stupid mom! Once she found out about you and Alyssa, she said that was it. She said you're a bad influence on me. I couldn't hang out with you guys anymore. She even made me get a different job. She made me promise to ignore you in school, too. If my brothers ever caught me talking to you, they'd tell her. I just know it."

I couldn't help but feel sorry for him. Evan was usually such a happy guy. Listening to him, I realized how broken up he really felt.

"I finally had enough," he continued. "I told my mom I didn't care anymore. I miss you and Alyssa too much. I mean, my mom grounded me for life basically, but it was worth it."

I chuckled briefly, just thinking of Evan trying to stand up to his scary mom.

"Have you heard what happened to Alyssa?" I asked him.

He nodded. "I actually called her on my way

over to see you. She and I came up with a plan."

"A plan for what?" I asked.

"A plan to fight her school on this," he replied.

I looked at him eagerly. "Well, tell me!"

"Well, now that she's had to time calm down, she got to thinking. I reminded her of all the laws and court cases she's read about. All of it is up in her head. Surely there's something she can use against them. The school suspending her because of the pregnancy is illegal. They're just using the fight as a cover—an excuse, even—to suspend her."

We continued to talk throughout the night. We played our game, too. For a few hours, my life felt normal again. I hadn't felt like that in months.

I don't think Evan realized how much that meant to me.

CHAPTER **SIXTEEN**

Alyssa asked me to come over the night before her school hearing. The kitchen table was filled with her law and history books. She sat typing at her laptop. I stayed up with her all night. None of us could sleep, anyway. Sometimes she'd ask me to run to the printer. I happily did so. Then she had me highlight and circle tons of information. It all looked so confusing. She was confident, though. Her research was on point.

She just wasn't confident the school would listen.

I looked at Alyssa almost sadly. Graduation was two weeks away. This should've been the time of our lives. Alyssa should have been excited, but here she was. Worried about school hearings. Worried about if we had saved up enough money for the baby. We should have been out there celebrating with our friends and families!

All of our classmates were looking forward to

college. Buying homes. Building families of their own. For them, that was years down the road. For me and Alyssa, a lot of that was being done right now.

At some point, her stepmom came downstairs. She looked at us lovingly. "Did you two sleep at all?" she asked. We both shook our heads, and then I realized that sunlight was shining through the window.

We had worked all through the night. I was used to that, I guess. It's all I was doing for the past nine months. We started clearing the table as the smell of coffee filled the house. All of us got ready to sit down to eat breakfast.

Well, except for Alyssa. She wanted to go through everything one more time.

"Please, just take a break," I told her. "If not for yourself then at least for the baby."

Alyssa didn't hesitate any longer. She closed her laptop and joined us for breakfast.

The bell ran as we entered Alyssa's school. The hallway was crowded. Some girls looked at us. They noticed Alyssa. Some of them whispered to each other. Some of them stared. Some even pointed at me, curiously. I can't believe this is what she'd been dealing with for months.

Alyssa's moms led the way toward the office.

I suddenly felt nervous. Alyssa, though, walked

tall. She held her hand over her belly, protectively. She didn't even flinch as we marched past everyone. Once we stepped into the office, though, I could sense something different.

Alyssa seemed to be a little nervous, and then the tears started. "I just want all of this to be over," she cried into my shoulder. Both of her moms helped her sit down in a chair.

I approached the front desk alone. "We're here for a hearing," I told the secretary. She didn't say a word to me. She pointed to a clipboard on the side of the desk. I wasn't even finished signing all of our names when the office door opened.

Principal Stewart appeared. "You're five minutes late," she told Alyssa. There was no emotion on her face. Just an impatient tone in her voice.

Everyone nervously stood up and headed for the principal's office. Everyone else entered before me, and then Principal Stewart held her arm across the door. "You, sir," she told me. "You have to wait out here."

I looked at Alyssa and her parents. They looked at me, and then they looked up at Principal Stewart. There was pure anger on their faces.

"He has every right to be here for her," Alyssa's mother said sternly.

The principal rolled her eyes. She looked

up and down at me. I could feel it. Her judging eyes. "So you must be the father, then," she said, almost in disgust. Her voice seemed to roll its eyes. "They get younger all the time."

I was over this lady already. She dropped her arm from across the door, pointing into her office. I made my way in. As I walked, I felt her breath on the back of my neck.

A long table sat in the middle of the office. Eight people were sitting on one side. They all had name tags and titles. They were teachers, board members, and assistant principals. Alyssa was told to take a seat across from them. We were directed to sit in the chairs against the wall.

Some board members began whispering to each other. I don't think they realized just how pregnant Alyssa was.

One of the assistant principals started by reading a prepared statement. School rules. School safety. Good student conduct. Being a responsible member of the community.

Alyssa sat there. I knew she was just pretending to listen. Pretending to care. She waited until they were finished, and then she opened up a red folder she had on her lap.

"Can I have my turn now?" she asked them. Principal Stewart nearly scoffed. "For weeks, I was bullied by a student on *your* Student Council.

For weeks, I asked someone to help."

One of the teachers raised her hand. "And we did step in," she said. "We took care of the issue."

"Except you didn't." Alyssa replied. She didn't shout or yell. She held her ground. "You removed her from the Student Council, but you did nothing to make sure that I was okay. You did nothing to make sure that the bullying stopped."

The board members didn't seem too bothered by it.

"And then," she continued, "the following day, she and five of her friends confronted me in the hallway. I was pushed up against my locker. I had every right to fight back to protect myself and my child."

Everyone at the table took notes. They didn't show any sign of emotion, just like Principal Stewart.

"People saw the fight, and they say you acted first," Principal Stewart said. "You wanted to get back at her for starting rumors. It all adds up."

"Except that's not what happened at all," Alyssa replied. "You would know that if you had watched the tape."

Just the *mention* of that tape made the room even quieter. Principal Stewart glared at Alyssa. "You have cameras in every corner of this school. I know that fight is on tape," Alyssa went on.

Principal Stewart laughed uncomfortably. She mumbled something. "The tapes," she said, "are too blurry. We can't make anything out."

Alyssa kept pressing the issue. "I believe I'm in my right to ask to see the tape for myself. Or, even better, see the tape with everyone here."

Principal Stewart suddenly looked tense. She told the board: "Let's move on!"

And they did.

Principal Stewart began reading a detailed list out loud. Dates of Alyssa's absences and late arrivals. All the times she had to leave class to see the nurse. The board members listened. Alyssa did too. I swear—that girl didn't even blink at them.

Alyssa pulled out a large envelope from her folder. "Here are all of my notes," she stated. "Every note from every one of my doctor's visits. I personally handed in copies to the main office. So where did they disappear to?"

Principal Stewart pretended not to hear. She continued reading. Finally, she stopped. "With this in mind," Principal Stewart said, "we need to make a decision. We need to decide whether or not this... very young... and very *pregnant* girl... will be joining us on graduation day."

Alyssa was ready to strike back.

She took out ten stapled packets of paper from her folder. She stacked them all up neatly on the table in front of her. And then, very coolly, she slid a copy across the table to every board member.

Some looked curiously at their packet. Others looked surprised. One started to wipe sweat from her forehead, and Principal Stewart's jaw dropped. She looked to each side to see the reactions from everyone. The room fell absolutely silent as they read what was in front of them.

And Alyssa. With a smile, she directed them to look at every line she had me highlight.

Alyssa began listing off every law. Every court case. *Everything* that protected pregnant students like her. And then she listed every school that had tried—and failed—to silence students in similar situations.

"You can't punish me because I'm *pregnant.*"

The board members all looked at each other for a moment. They closed their notebooks. Principal Stewart knew that was it. One of the assistant principals stood up. "I believe we owe you an apology, Ms. Holbrook," she said.

She then promised a full investigation into the girl who started the fight. They also promised Alyssa that she could return to school. *Immediately.* She would be able to walk across the stage for graduation.

Principal Stewart put her face into her hands. We had won.

CHAPTER**SEVENTEEN**

Alyssa walked across the stage just weeks later. Proudly. More pregnant than ever. The baby was due any day.

And me? I graduated the day after her.

We both decided that we'd throw one big graduation party. Our parents weren't too sure, though. "Please. It'll save everybody time. And money. Two things nobody has enough of right now," Alyssa told our parents. They agreed, reluctantly.

Alyssa did ask for one thing. "My dad! I want him there, too."

Her moms couldn't say no this time. It was her graduation party, after all. Little did Alyssa know that I had already reached out to him. I figured she'd want her dad around for when the baby arrived.

I almost told her mom in private, but then her mom suddenly went off. "He's always trying to outdo me!" she yelled. I knew from the stories that he was her *ex*-husband for a reason. I ended up telling Alyssa's stepmother instead. She was happy to hear it.

We had the party in my backyard. Evan was the first one to arrive—four hours early. He asked where we needed help. "How about you clean out the pool for us?" my dad asked. So Evan did, and then he stayed in it for the rest of the day. Well, until the cake came out, at least.

The party was a lot of fun. The weather was perfect. We had more food than we could possibly eat, and Alyssa was getting a lot of attention from both of our families. Maybe too much attention.

I was talking to Alyssa during dinner when her mom suddenly got very quiet. Alyssa looked up and screamed—her dad had made it. Alyssa wiped happy tears from her eyes.

In all my years knowing Alyssa, I'd never met her dad. He was different than I expected. Alyssa looked just like him. The first thing he did was thank me for reaching out to him. He was so friendly. Alyssa was smiling from ear to ear.

"This kid," he said to Alyssa as he put his arm around my shoulder. "He's a keeper."

He then told us both, "Oh! And my gift to the two of you. Well, the *three* of you, actually," he said. "My company just fixed up a nice little apartment downtown. It's close to a couple of the schools over there. And I thought, 'You know, it's just the right size for a small family.' I want you two to have it. Live your life. Raise that kid. And please, just stay in school." I couldn't believe it. Things had been *hard*, but we had so much support, and I know most people in this situation weren't so lucky.

I heard Alyssa's mother nearly choke on her hamburger. She excused herself from the picnic table. "See!" she cried. "He's always outdoing me!"

The party began winding down. We started saying our goodbyes to everyone. Alyssa was sitting with her dad when he called me over. He told me to sit down. Just for a moment.

"You two," he said, almost in a whisper. "You're still just kids *yourselves*. But you're great kids. Everyone who was here tonight knows that. Just promise me you'll both stay happy. In a few days, nothing else is going to matter except that baby."

Alyssa and I both locked eyes. In that moment, I felt something change in Alyssa. Things were never the same between us after that.

CHAPTER **EIGHTEEN**

In the middle of one balmy night in June, Alyssa's mom called me. My parents and I raced to the hospital. I don't know how we didn't get a ticket.

Alyssa had a hard time during labor. She screamed and cried and needed more pain meds than she'd thought. I had a hard time just watching it all.

And then she was here. A girl. Baby Sara was finally here, after all those months. She had a head full of black hair, just like me. Her cheeks were perfectly round. And her blue eyes! They were just like her mother's.

We made sure we held her before anyone else got a chance. Our parents couldn't get enough of Sara Ann. She was perfect. Laura, though, wasn't amused. "That's it?" she asked us.

Evan showed up later that evening with flowers and balloons. One balloon read

"GET WELL SOON." The other read "IT'S A

BOY!" I took one look at Evan and shook my head.

"Really, Evan!?" I asked. Evan laughed.

"This is all they had! It cost me like fifteen dollars in the gift shop!"

Later that night, me and Alyssa sat up with the baby. "I can't believe she's finally here," Alyssa said. She held Sara close to her chest.

"It's definitely been an adventure," I replied. "But it was worth it. Wasn't it?"

Alyssa didn't respond for a moment. She was lost in thought, looking into Sara's eyes.

"We did the right thing. Didn't we?" she asked. I looked at her. She looked like she was about to cry. "I mean, we gave up *everything*. College. Careers. Just so we could go through this all. For us. For *her*."

Sara suddenly started to cry. "Rest," I told Alyssa as I gently picked up the baby. Alyssa quietly thanked me. I calmed Sara down after minute or two. By the time I turned back, Alyssa was sound asleep.

CHAPTER NINETEEN

Six months later, it was Sara's first Christmas Eve. Alyssa brought her to my parents' house. Sara met lots of my family and she showed off lots of new skills. She loved rolling onto her stomach and creeping across the floor. Everyone would get so excited for her. Sara would just coo and smile.

I made Evan honorary uncle the day Sara was born. He helped me babysit sometimes. And by babysit, I mean read a bunch of comics to her. Sara fell asleep to them. I couldn't blame her for that. The pictures, though. She loved the colorful pictures.

Evan came over that Christmas Eve and played a bit with Sara. My mom teased him. "You're a natural, Evan," she said.

Evan's eyes got real wide. "Yeah, no," he told her. "I'm good until I'm forty, at *least*."

Sara was beyond spoiled that day. She had more toys than I knew what to do with, and I knew Santa would be bringing her even more tomorrow.

It was a perfectly happy and normal Christmas Eve. That was kind of the point.

Eventually, Alyssa and I politely began excusing ourselves for the night. My parents both pulled me aside as I put on my boots. "We're proud of you, Bryan," my dad said. "Don't ever forget that. And call us if you need *anything*."

I promised to do that as I gave them the biggest hug.

I held Sara as we went outside. The streetlights gave us just enough light.

Alyssa went to her car and came back a minute later. She helped get the car seat into my car. Once Sara was strapped in, Alyssa kissed her goodbye. "Promise you'll be good for Daddy. I'll see you tomorrow night." Alyssa then stood up and looked at me. "Got everything you need?" she asked. I nodded my head.

"My new apartment's all set," I said. "Evan even helped babyproof everything. But he hid all my forks and knives! And he won't tell me where he hid them. I've been eating everything with a spoon."

Alyssa cracked a smile. We said a quiet goodbye to each other.

Alyssa watched as we drove away. Sara was cooing to herself, but she got quieter and quieter. The drive into the city was slow. I drove extra carefully in the snow.

"Rides in the car make me sleepy, too," I told her. I was always tired, though, between night classes and working full-time. Mr. Jennings found out about Sara. He told me I should have said something sooner, and suddenly he realized why I knew so much about parenting books. He made me a manager. I then rehired Evan immediately.

For Alyssa and me, work and college classes proved to be too much. We tried so hard to make it work for five months. We took turns getting up to feed Sara. Change Sara. Hold Sara. We fell behind for a little while in school, and then we fell behind with each other.

We reached a tipping point at Thanksgiving. After dinner that night, I asked Alyssa what was wrong. She hadn't spoken to me all day.

"What my dad told us at our graduation party... I want to be happy. But these past few months are proof. I'm just not happy being with you right now, with all this."

As much as it hurt, I knew it had been coming. We promised to stay friends. Everyone says that, though. The damage was done. We did, however, agree to work together for Sara. And we were, even though it was the hardest thing I'd ever done.

I pulled into my apartment driveway. I grabbed bags of clothes, diapers, and gifts from the trunk. As soon as I went to get Sara, I could smell it. She needed to be changed, and badly!

I struggled to open the door as I held Sara in one arm. She was asleep. I tried so hard to be quiet. As soon as I turned on a light, my phone rang, and it was *loud*.

Sara woke up *screaming*. I still had bags sitting on the porch. And Sara's diaper! It was getting worse. I didn't know where to start.

Evan's name appeared on the screen. I put it on speaker. He heard Sara screaming in the background.

"I can call you back!" he said.

"Don't worry about it," I told him. "I'm just trying to figure everything out." I brought the bags in from the porch. I pulled a diaper out of one bag. I frantically searched for the wipes. They were buried in another bag. Sara continued screaming.

"I'm so sorry, baby," I told her. "Daddy's still learning! And besides, it's our first time alone together overnight."

"You've got this, Bryan," Evan reassured me over the phone. "Remember that giraffe that I made you change?" he asked. "Just picture that giraffe right now, okay?"

"But it's my *daughter*!" I shouted. Evan laughed.

"You're wasting time, Bryan. My timer's counting down. Go!"

WANT TO KEEP READING?

If you liked this book, check out another book
from West 44 Books:

THE WATER YEAR
BY MAX HOWARD

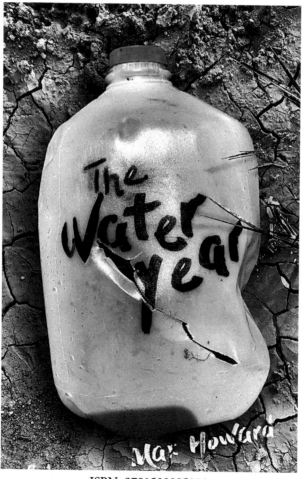

ISBN: 9781538385111

Chapter 1

Dear Mom,

Lucas Ross is a dung heap with a tongue ring. How is my best friend in love with him?

He gets Doritos stuck in his braces. He clicks his tongue ring against his teeth when other people are talking.

Amy and I usually see eye to eye, but whenever Lucas raises his dumb eyebrows, she laughs. He's always raising his eyebrows. Or else he repeats what you say in a sarcastic voice. He's like a walking meme.

A mean meme.

The worst part is, I hardly ever see Amy anymore.

I miss her.

And you.

Love,
Sophie

"Sophie, you *have* to go to the Sato twins' Fall Bash," Amy says. She swirls her french fries in ketchup. Her boyfriend, Lucas, nuzzles her neck. "Pretty please? I never get to *see* you anymore."

"I don't know. It's weird the party's on a weeknight," Sophie says. She looks down at her lunch. Limp, slimy school pizza slumps on her tray. "I have to go study for my history quiz."

Lucas slides his mouth off Amy's neck. "Uh, Sophie? What's a *weeknight*?"

His voice is serious, but his face is mocking. He clicks his tongue ring against his teeth.

"You know. Like a school night," Sophie says.

"Here's the thing: I don't think *weeknights* exist," Lucas declares.

"He's right," Amy pipes up. "The days of the week are just a social construct. You know. Just something humans made up."

"Weekends are as made-up as Santa Claus," Lucas says. He crunches a fry. "You don't still believe in Santa, do you?"

"I have to go," Sophie says. *Santa might not exist,* she thinks. *But Mr. Orr is a real bear. History quizzes are the worst.*

"Come to the party. There's going to be a bonfire. In the desert! On a full moon," Amy says.

"A full *blood moon*," Lucas adds.

"If you come with us, I'll sleep over Friday *and* Saturday. I'll help you take care of Violet," Amy promises.

"Who's Violet?" says Lucas.

"Sophie's sister," says Amy. "She's in second grade. She's so cute. She's obsessed with that cartoon movie—*Ice Fairies.*"

"That cartoon one about the fairy princesses? With the song about snow—"

Amy and Sophie burst out singing "Here I Am," the hit song from *Ice Fairies.*

Lucas scoffs. "I can't believe you guys like that princess stuff."

"It's about sisters who rescue each other!" Amy says. "And there's no kiss at the end. It's feminist!"

Lucas shrugs. "Is it feminist? Or are they just trying to sell little girls T-shirts?"

"And tutus," Sophie says.

"What?" says Lucas.

"Yeah," says Amy. "They sell tutus, too."

"Violet *only* wears *Ice Fairies* T-shirts and tutus," Sophie says.

"Whatever," says Lucas. "Let's focus. Sophie. You going to the party?" He clicks his tongue ring, making a tick-tock sound.

Yuck. Imagine driving to the party with Lucas and Amy. How long would the car ride be? Would his tongue click the whole way?

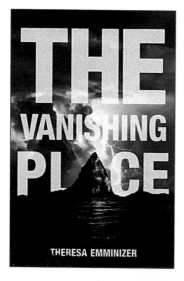

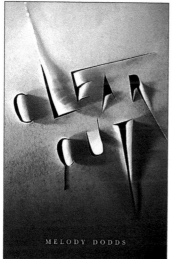

CHECK OUT MORE BOOKS AT:
www.west44books.com

An imprint of Enslow Publishing

WEST **44** BOOKS™

ABOUT THE AUTHOR

P.A. Kurch is a writer and teacher from Buffalo, New York. He is also an avid videogame fan and collector of all things geeky - which lovingly made their way into this book. This is his second novel for young adults, after having released *Knights of Suburbia* in 2019.